This book is lovingly dedicated to our grandchildren.

ISBN: 0-9722570-0-4

Published by

Snowbound
BOOKS™

www.deertales.com

Book design by Julie Melton, The Right Type Graphics (USA)

Printed in Hong Kong

2nd printing, 2003

Pogonip Magic

Story by Karen Collett Wilson

Photography by Susan A. Zerga

Susan Zerga

Did I ever tell you the story of the magic that blew through our Cottonwoods last winter? Gather near, and I'll tell you what happened.

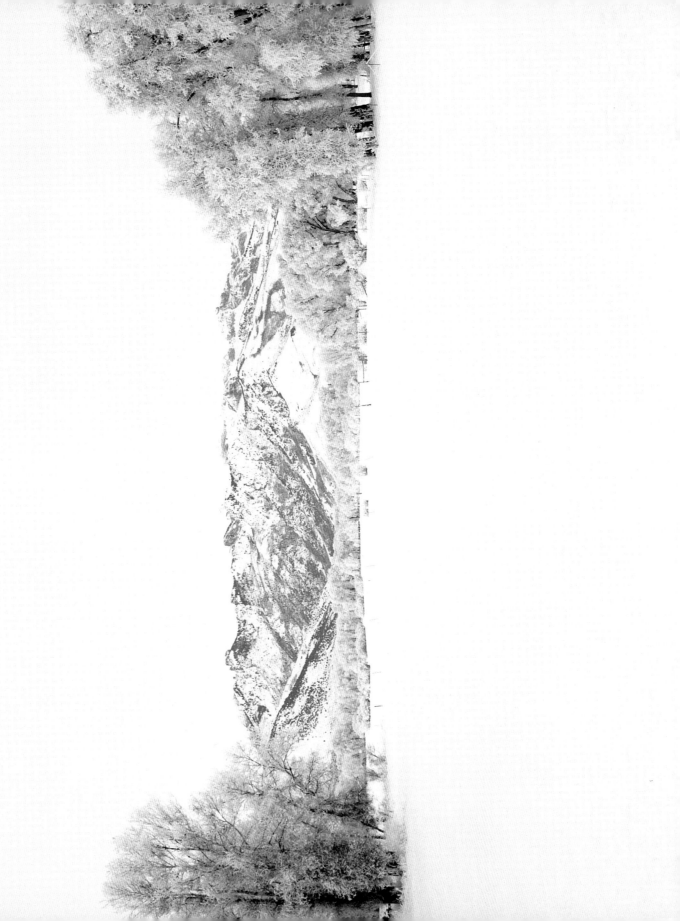

It was a bone-chilling winter's dawn. There was snow on the ground and, of course, there were no leaves on the trees.

But, on that special morning, all the bare branches were outlined with pogonip. (*Pogonip is a Native American word for a frost that appears when conditions are just right. It turns winter's bare, brown branches into a white fairy-land.*)

The entire woods were covered with the thick, twinkling frost. It looked magical!

Well, on that beautiful, frosty morning the animals in the Cottonwoods did just what they always did on a cold winter morning. They stretched, then came out from their warm burrows or from their protective bushes or trees.

Many animals lived in the Cottonwoods. There were rabbits and porcupines. There were badgers and raccoons and skunks. But the rulers of the Cottonwoods were the deer. The stately, graceful, haughty deer were the royalty of the woods.

All of the other animals bowed and moved out of the way when they came near. The deer did not play with the other animals, or even talk to them. They were very stuck-up!

On that sparkling pogonip morning, the deer, too, woke up as usual, but while they stretched, a soft breeze began to move through the trees. It picked up the frost from the branches and sprinkled it into the air. Then the soft breeze swirled the glittery air all around the deer.

(That's when something strange happened!)

Remember, how stuck-up those deer were, how they ignored the other animals in the Cottonwoods? Well, at the moment that the pogonip touched their backs and antlers, they looked up and saw their animal neighbors and smiled at them. (Did you know that deer could smile?) They even said, "Good morning!" (and they'd never said that before!)

It was then that the wandering cat appeared in the Cottonwoods. The cat was very tired and very cold. He could hardly walk another step. He saw the deer and immediately began to bow.

But the leader of the herd did an amazing thing.
He stepped forward and said, "You look tired and
cold, and we would like to help you."

Another of the noble deer moved closer and bowed his crown of antlers to the cold and tired visitor.

Then he softly blew his warming breath on the cat . . . .

...and licked him with his warming tongue.

The cat closed his tired eyes and purred his thanks.

Later, rested and warmed, the wandering cat continued on his way.

To this day, nobody quite knows what happened in those sparkling woods. There was pogonip. There was a soft breeze. There was a wandering cat. And, there were deer who behaved as they never had before… or since.

I think it was magic!